For Lionel Richard Sanders
1936 - 2016
Thank you for filling my childhood with tire swings, fishing
holes, and daily lessons of acceptance. Your constant
examples of compassion and zero tolerance for bullying
were the inspiration for this story.

# LET'S SPREAD THE MESSAGE THAT WEIRD IS WONDERFUL!

## FOLLOW @LITTLELEMONBOOK ON INSTAGRAM AND USE #ICHOOSEWEIRD!

ISBN-13: 9780986262128
Published by Little Lemon Production House
Written by Karen Sanders-Betts
Illustrated and Designed by Hannah Howerton
Copyright © 2015
Made in PRC
www.thelittlelemonthatleapt.com
www.facebook.com/littlelemonbook
Instagram/Twitter: @littlelemonbook
#ichooseweird

# THE LITTLE LEMON THAT LEAPT

WRITTEN BY KAREN SANDERS-BETTS | ILLUSTRATED BY HANNAH HOWERTON

## STARRING LIONEL THE LEMON

**MOTHER/DAUGHTER →**
**AUTHOR/ILLUSTRATOR**

Karen Sanders-Betts and Hannah Howerton are a mother/daughter team who share a love for lattes, live theater, and bringing laughter to life's seemingly ordinary moments. Karen received her bachelor's degree in journalism and minor in English from the University of Central Missouri, and Hannah received her bachelor's degree in political science and minor in history of art from UC Berkeley. Together they created 'The Little Lemon that Leapt,' their uniquely unique children's book that encourages kids to embrace what makes them (and the rest of this mesmerizing world) weird.

It all began with a sentence in Karen's notebook: the little lemon leapt without fear. From that, Karen and Hannah chose to leap together, combining their dreams into one reality. The story itself is imaginative, quirky, and fun; a little lemon who thinks he is normal leaps from his tree, only to discover the whole world is weird and so is he. The alliteration and illustrations alone make the story a must have for every child's bookshelf, but the underlying message of embracing differences in yourself and in others is what sets 'The Little Lemon that Leapt' apart.

The message was inspired by Karen's father, Lionel, who filled her childhood with daily lessons of acceptance. His legacy lives on through Lionel the Lemon. When Karen and Hannah started their business, they said that if they made a difference in one child's life it would be worth it. After hearing feedback from countless parents and teachers, it is clear they have surpassed their goal. This isn't just about a book. It is about a movement to raise a generation of children who are full of compassion and empathy, and who choose to celebrate what makes them WEIRD! #ichooseweird

**ENOUGH ABOUT YOU! LET'S START MY STORY!**

This lemon wasn't uniquely unique,
or especially special.
He lacked a particular flair,
LIKE
SLAMMING
POETRY
...

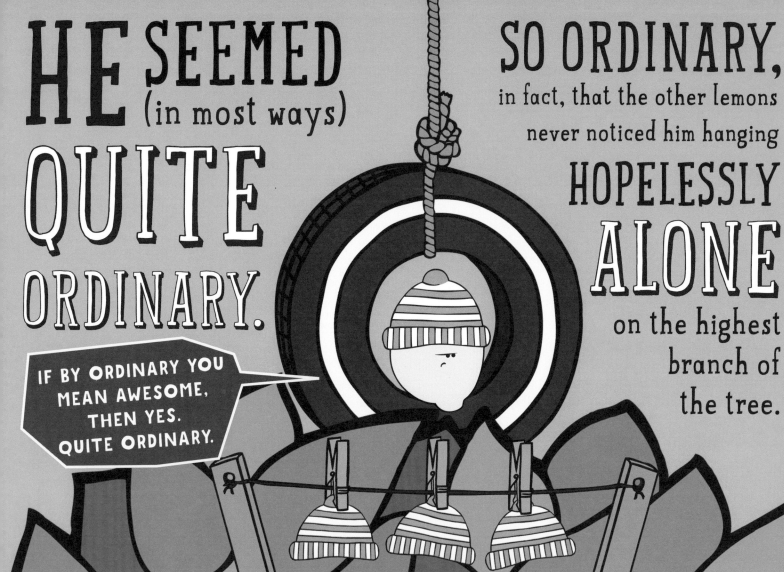

They were **TOO BUSY** discussing more important things like **LEMON MERINGUE PIE, LEMON CURD,** and **LEMONADE.** The little lemon didn't join their curious conversations, or share their **DISTURBING DREAMS.**

From the tip top of the tree, the little lemon could SEE THE WORLD. It was a MAGNIFICENT, MARVELOUS, MESMERIZING WORLD, and the little lemon longed to be part of it.

He was deep in a daydream when a
**BUMBLEBEE BUZZED BY**
with a bundle of balloons and nearly
knocked him right off the tree.

**"HEY, WATCH IT!"**
the little lemon cried out.
**"WAIT, WHERE ARE YOU GOING?"**

The busy bee did not answer.
He had places to go.
The little lemon wanted to go places too.
He was sick of being stuck in a tree.

That is when he had (by far)
his best idea of the day:

# HE HAD TO LEAP!

His perfect plan had
ONE teeny, tiny, tangle:

## LEMONS. DON'T. LEAP.

Lemons hang and hover, they even
dangle, droop, and drop;
BUT NEVER EVER,
IN THE HISTORY OF TIME EVER,
had a lemon ever leapt.

# LUCKILY,
the little lemon
did not know this.

DIDN'T
KNOW
WHAT?

# THE TREMENDOUS TREE SHOOK AND SWAYED

as the little lemon burst from its boughs
with a positively petrifying

LEAPING
LEMONS!
HE'S
LOST HIS
MIND!

## POP!

WOO
HOOOOO!

Dazed lemons by
the dozens watched with
**DREAD** and **DISBELIEF**
as the little lemon

## LEAPT!

UH OH...I'M FEELING A BIT WOOZY

Pulling off a picture perfect landing, he gave the suitably shocked lemons a single salute and set off to SEE the WORLD.

He hadn't gone far (not far at all) when he found himself head to head with a

# HUFFY HEDGEHOG.

"**EXCUSE ME,**" said the little lemon, "**WHAT ARE YOU DOING?**"

The hedgehog **HURRIEDLY** hammered away. "Hanging a banner for my bluegrass band's PREMIERE PERFORMANCE," he replied.

The little lemon howled with laughter.
"Hedgehogs snuffle and snort, they even puff and pop,
but they DEFINITELY DON'T SING BLUEGRASS!"

"THIS ONE DOES!"
the harried hedgehog
HUFFED.
"I AM READY TO
REHEARSE.
NOW GO AWAY."
So the little lemon
(sorta sadly)
WENT AWAY.

OH, AND I SUPPOSE BEARS DON'T BANG BANJOS?

He was still wondering about the weirdness of a hedgehog singing with a banjo banging bear when a

FIERY FLASH FILLED THE FOREST.

Bewildered by what it could be, the little lemon headed hastily toward the light.

THIS IS MY BEWILDERED FACE.

Through the trees, a **FASTIDIOUSLY FASHIONABLE FOX** was photographing a **RAKISH ROOSTER.**

"Excuse me, what are you doing?" asked the little lemon.

"I am taking a portrait of my **FINE FEATHERED FRIEND,**" the persnickety fox purred.

"Foxes can't be friends with roosters!" the little lemon said sassily.

**"FOXES EAT ROOSTERS!"**

**FACE FLUSHED,**
the little lemon took two steps back.
**THE FOX** QUICKLY
FOLLOWED.

# "NO?"

## HE QUIPPED.

"Then I suggest that you GO AWAY."

So for the second time
that day, the little lemon
# (QUITE QUICKLY)
went away.

"I AM PROPERLY PACKED AND PREPARING TO FLY TO PARIS FOR CULINARY CLASSES," the penguin pompously replied.

THIS DAY JUST GOT A 'LATTE' WEIRDER.

Gasping through giggles, THE LITTLE LEMON finally found his voice; "PENGUINS CAN'T COOK! HEY, PENGUINS CAN'T EVEN FLY!"

For the third time that day, the little lemon (SOMEWHAT SOURLY) WENT AWAY.

"What a weird world," he said to himself.

HEY! A DIME!

↑10¢

It wasn't long, not long at all, before he stumbled upon a CURIOUS CONTRAPTION.

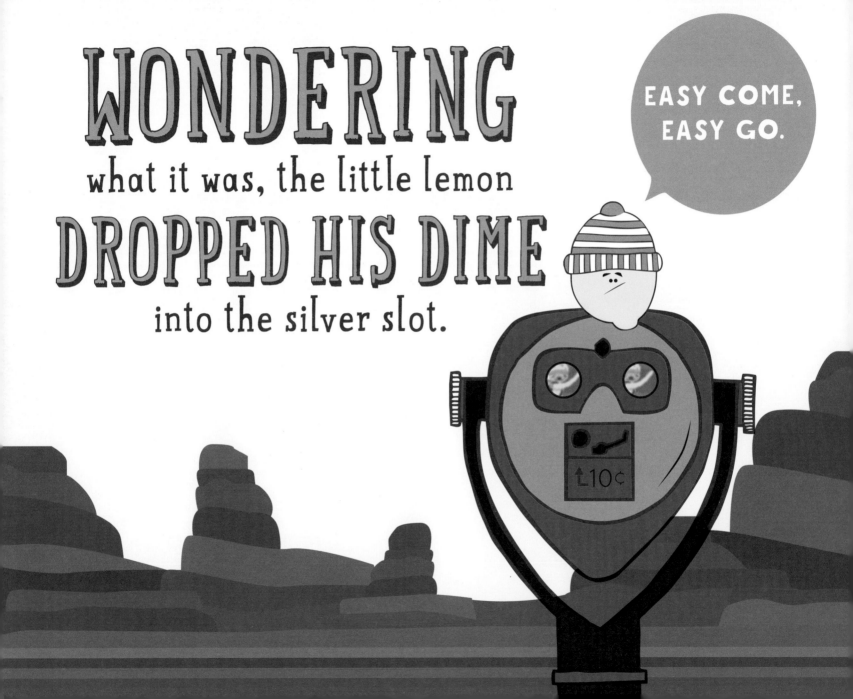

Through the
**MECHANICAL MAGNIFIER,**
he spied a
**SPORTY SLOTH**
in sneakers
hoisting himself
up a
**HOODOO.**

"WHAT ARE YOU DOING UP THERE?" the little lemon bellowed.

"CLIMBING TO THE CREST!"
the sporty sloth bellowed back.

Lesson STILL not learned,
the little lemon's laughter
echoed up the rugged rocks.

↑10¢

"SLOTHS DON'T CLIMB ROCKS!" he called out.
"SLOTHS BARELY EVEN BUDGE!"

"THIS ONE DOES!"

the scaling sloth snapped.

"I AM CLEARLY CONCENTRATING. NOW GO AWAY!"

So for the fourth time that day,

the little lemon

(rather reluctantly)

went away.

Feeling frustrated and in need
of a nap, the little lemon
was happy to happen upon a

# TIDY TEPEE.

He was
## ALMOST ASLEEP
when a pop of pink appeared. A
## BRAWNY BUFFALO
in a
# PINK TUTU
was dancing around the tiny tepee!

## "WHAT ARE YOU DOING?"
yawned the sleepy little lemon.

TWIRLING AS HE TALKED,
the buffalo briskly replied,
"PRACTICING MY
PIROUETTES!"

SNORT HUFF GRUNT

This gave the little lemon (by far)
his BIGGEST laugh of the day.
"Buffaloes don't dance,
and ballet is for GIRLS!"

The big bull stopped spinning.
"THIS ONE DOES, BEANIE BOY!"

"NOW GO AWAY!"

So for the FIFTH time that day,
the little lemon (a touch terrified,
and a bit hurt by the beanie
comment) went away...

**CATCH ME IF YOU CAN,
TUTU BOY!**

# CHASED

(of course) by the big bull buffalo in his petal pink tutu as the world whirled by.

**THIS BEANIE WAS BUILT FOR SPEED!**

**HE RAN** (AND HE RAN) UNTIL HE RAN right into the long leg of a **GINORMOUS GIRAFFE.**

The little lemon looked high into the sky. "WHAT ARE YOU DOING UP THERE?" he hollered.

The ginormous giraffe **CRUNCHED AND MUNCHED.** "Enjoying a leisurely lunch," he said briefly between bites.

CRUNCH

MUNCH

CRUNCH

MUNCH

**"SOMEONE NORMAL!"**

the little lemon exclaimed excitedly. "I was beginning to believe the **WHOLE WORLD** was **WEIRD!"**

The crunching and munching suddenly stopped. **"WEIRD? Why?"** the ginormous giraffe asked.

**"BECAUSE,"**

the frustrated little lemon blurted, "hedgehogs AREN'T SUPPOSED to be in bands, roosters should RUN from foxes, penguins can't cook (OR FLY), sloths should STAY PUT, buffaloes **DEFINITELY DON'T DANCE BALLET..."**

L+C

The ginormous giraffe gently interjected: "And lemons don't leap."

# "YEAH!"

the little lemon almost agreed, "and lemons don't...wait...WHAT?"
The little lemon looked a WEE BIT WORRIED.
"This one did," he said hesitantly. "Does that make ME weird?"

# THE GINORMOUS GIRAFFE

swiftly swooped to the little lemon's level.

## "ABSOLUTELY!"

he said with a wise wink,
"and weird is (by far) my favorite."

For the first time that day, the little
lemon saw what makes the world

## MAGNIFICENT, MARVELOUS,
## AND MESMERIZING.

Everyone is a little bit weird,
and THAT is what makes them wonderful.

The ginormous giraffe nudged his new friend. "Do you want to go back to the tree, or would you rather **EXPLORE** the rest of this **WEIRD WORLD?**" Lesson learned, the little lemon smiled. **"I CHOOSE WEIRD!"**